GROSSET & DUNLAP
An Imprint of Penguin Random House LLC, New York

Text by Hannah Sheldon-Dean

Visit us online at www.penguinrandomhouse.com.

Library of Congress Cataloging-in-Publication Data is available upon request.

ISBN 9781524792091   10 9 8 7 6 5 4 3 2 1

ROALD DAHL

DREAM BIG

and Other Life Lessons from
THE ENORMOUS CROCODILE

illustrated by Quentin Blake

Grosset & Dunlap

LIFE ISN'T EASY.
Especially when you're a child-eating crocodile.

Sometimes it feels like the whole world is telling you to settle for less than you **DESERVE.**

But with some **clever** tricks, you can learn to seize opportunities

and hang on to the beauty in life.

Sometimes, it's best to
fake it till you make it.

Other times, you've just got to roll with the punches.

REMEMBER,
life truly is one big balancing act.

But the key is to surround yourself with people

who lift
you up . . .

. . . and find **friends** who aren't afraid to leave their **comfort zones**.

Even if you're not sure you'll

FIT IN . . .

. . . DREAM BIG

and grab every chance to
sink your teeth into
better things.

CONFIDENCE
is a virtue.

Never be **afraid** to take
your place at the table . . .

. . . and always go after

what you really
WANT.

AND REMEMBER

if you always reach

for the stars . . .

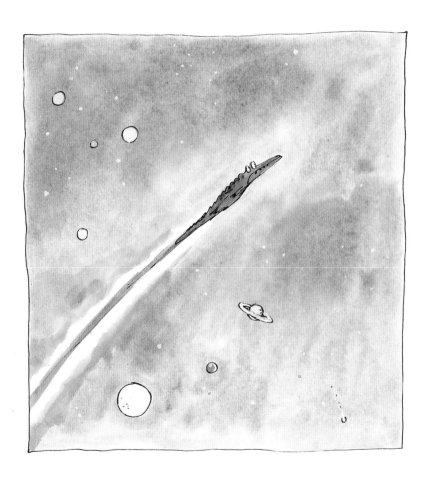

. . . you just might
find your place
in the SUN!